WAG
AND THE SECRETS OF
BOW-WOW

RAYMOND PAUL BOYD

To order additional copies of this book, contact:
Xlibris
844-714-8691
www.Xlibris.com
Orders@Xlibris.com

ISBN: Softcover 978-1-6641-6941-8
ISBN: EBook 978-1-6641-6940-1

Print information available on the last page

Rev. date: 07/13/2021

Published Titles

The Alpha Dracula
The Presidents Wife
It's Who You Know
The Log Cabin
The Shadow of Paradise
E-mail to Heaven
The Judgement of Sarah Solomon
Condemnation
Laraine Day FBI
Puppy in the White House
WAG to the Rescue

DEDICATION

In loving memory of my wife, Gloria, who enjoyed the written word of fantasy and for the young hearts. I also dedicate this to my daughters, Paula Boyd and Cynthia Levy and to my son Larry Boyd.

INTRODUCTION

Wag, once again was the main attraction in the animals heavenly kingdom. He stood on the stage in the great hall. All of his fellow creatures anxiously waited to hear why Wag, sought an audience with the all knowing Bow-Wow, whom magically appeared on the stage. Radiating in splendor all applauded after a moment he raised his right paw, and bow his head slightly in acknowledgement of their applause, and there was instant silence. Bow-Wow, then spoke saying forgive me sisters, and brothers for my delay. I have been visiting with our creator. He sends his love, and blessing to each of you. Bow-Wow, then turn his attention to Wag, asking how he could help? There was a twinkle in his eyes indicating that he was aware of the reason Wag, had wish to speak to him, but for the benefit of all in attendance, Bow-Wow. Allow Wag, to tell why he had wish to address the all knowing Bow-Wow, I have just return from earth, the fact is that our sisters, and brother our in need of help. They are weary, as we all are aware many of our sisters, and brothers are used for food. What I suggest O'great and wise one is that you return to earth with me. Bow-Wow, smiled and said, Wag, you do know that all on earth have been ordained by the creator to have a reason for their existence. But I shall return with you. Hug, the bear was the first to speak saying I also shall go. And so shall I said Chi-Chi, the monkey, Bow-Wow, replied saying he knew they all are eager to come, but that cannot be. Wag, was delighted for he thought the all knowing Bow-Wow, may had refused to go.

Magically in a blink of an eye Wag, and Bow-Wow, were standing by a pond there the animals came to quench their thirst in the middle of the African plains. The lions, and the cheetah, and other for some strange reason the weaker were not attack, and eaten. They all came in pairs male and female to Bow-Wow, knowing he had a message of hope for each of them.

In the animal heavenly kingdom, once again Wag was the main attraction as he stood on the stage of the great hall, as all his fellow-creatures anxiously awaited to hear and see why Wag sought an audience with the all-knowing Bow-wow.

Bow-wow stepped on to the stage radiating in splendor; he was applauded. After a moment, he raised his right paw and bowed his head slightly in acknowledgment of their cheers, and there was instant silence. He spoke, saying, "Forgive me, sisters and brothers, for being late. I have visited our creator. He sends his love and blessing to each of you, and he's proud of the good works of our comforters that are sent to earth to help all on the planet earth."

Bow-wow then turned his attention to Wag, asking, "How could I be of help?" There was a twinkle in his eyes indicating that he was aware of the reason why Wag asked to speak with him. But for the benefit of all, Bow-wow let Wag speak for his reason.

The zebra and his mate listened as Bow-wow spoke softly. Happily, they trotted away with a smile. Wag was unable to hear what Bow-wow had said.

Next came the impala with his mate. They were pleased to hear what Bow-wow had said too, as they walked away smiling. Wag was unable to hear Bow-wow's words.

The gazelle and his mate came next. They also were pleased with what Bow-wow had said as they skipped away, and yet Wag couldn't hear what Bow-wow said though he tried so hard to listen.

18

The elands also were thrilled to hear the spoken words of Bow-wow—joyous as they walked away. Even though Wag perked his ears, he didn't hear the spoken words of Bow-wow.

Next that was delighted to hear what Bow-wow had said were the two ostriches that flapped their wings as they happily ran away. Wag was still at a loss to hear what Bow-wow had said.

22

The mighty lion and his mate approached Bow-wow who was smiling and said, "I know you both are sorry." Wag put his paw into his right ear, moving it vigorously, wishing it might enhance his hearing, but to no avail, Wag was again at a loss to hear what Bow-wow had said.

The cheetah with his mate—their speed was unmatched. "You do not need to regret what you do to survive," Bow-wow said with authority. They, too, happily departed. Wag again, though he tried, hadn't heard what Bow-wow had said.

The two monkeys, holding hands, anxiously heard Bow-wow's words of solace; they, too, departed gleefully. Wag had listened intently, but still, he couldn't hear.

The bull elephant and his mate trumpeted happily having heard what Bow-wow had said as they walked away. Wag wondered if he should ask Bow-wow why everyone was so happy after he had spoken to them.

30

"Now is the time we should leave," Bow-wow said as he put his right paw into the water.

"Why did you do that?" Wag asked.

Bow-wow replied, saying, "During the next three days, all that drink of this water shall know what I have said."

32

A moment before they vanished from the African plains, Wag saw the sky darken with all manner of winged creatures flying down to the water hole.

"Where are we?" Wag asked.

Bow-wow replied, saying, "We are on a farm in New Jersey. Here I shall give my message before we return."

Just as Wag was about to ask what the message was, the boar with mother pig was next, and they, too, returned to their sty happy as to what the all-knowing Bow-wow had said. Wag again remained silent.

38

Next came the bull with mother cow. They departed happily. Wag since he would soon know what Bow-wow had been saying.

Last to hear what Bow-wow had to say were Mr. and Mrs. Duck. They waddled away quacking with joy.

Bow-wow told Wag the secret. As they were about to return to the heavenly kingdom, Bow-wow said to Wag, "I know you are anxious that I should tell you what I have said to our sisters and brothers."

"Oh yes, I am most anxious," replied Wag.

"All I said is that every living creature has a soul and that several moments before death, the body does not suffer pain because the soul leaves the body and returns to the creators heavenly kingdom of animals and their life continues."

And they all lived happily ever after.

The vacating of the soul is a fact of God's boundless love and mercy. I can attest to that. The proof of the existence of the soul I experience on March 16, 1966, at approximately 8:00 a.m., but that's another story.